Loyal Young

Communion. A Treatise on Christian Fellowship

Anatiposi

Loyal Young

Communion. A Treatise on Christian Fellowship

Reprint of the original.

1st Edition 2023 | ISBN: 978-3-38210-684-3

Anatiposi Verlag is an imprint of Outlook Verlagsgesellschaft mbH.

Verlag (Publisher): Outlook Verlag GmbH, Zeilweg 44, 60439 Frankfurt, Deutschland
Vertretungsberechtigt (Authorized to represent): E. Roepke, Zeilweg 44, 60439 Frankfurt, Deutschland
Druck (Print): Books on Demand GmbH, In de Tarpen 42, 22848 Norderstedt, Deutschland

COMMUNION.

A

TREATISE ON CHRISTIAN FELLOWSHIP

WITH

GOD AND HIS SAINTS.

BY THE

REV. LOYAL YOUNG, D.D.,

AUTHOR OF "COMMENTARY ON ECCLESIASTES," ETC.

PHILADELPHIA:

PRESBYTERIAN BOARD OF PUBLICATION,

1334 CHESTNUT STREET.

WESTCOTT & THOMSON,
Stereotypers, Philada.

TO

ALL THOSE WHO

LONG FOR MORE INTIMATE COM-

MUNION WITH GOD AND HIS PEOPLE, AND

ARE IN SYMPATHY WITH THAT SPIRIT OF FELLOW-

SHIP WHICH IS MORE AND MORE PERVAD-

ING THE CHRISTIAN WORLD, THIS

LITTLE WORK IS

DEDICATED,

BY ONE WHO DESIRES A HUMBLE PLACE

AMONG THEM, NOW, AND IN

GLORY.

PREFATORY.

THE law of communion or attraction pervades the universe. In inanimate things it is *attraction*, in rational and sentient beings it is *communion*. It exists in the grain of sand that seeks the bosom of the earth; in the bird gathering her nestlings under her wings; in the mother and child clasping each other in warm embrace; and in God stooping from his high abode to converse with and comfort his children, while his children with joy run to his arms and call him Father!

From the simplest form of attraction in mere matter, through all the upward grades of vegetable and animal organizations and instincts and human love and fellowship, this attraction is seen and felt. But infinitely higher, purer, more joyful, is the religious fellowship that binds the Christian's heart to his God and to his fellow-Christian. It is of this communion that we de-

1 *   5

sire to speak. It is this communion that we desire to know and experience.

O God of love, draw the heart of the writer and the heart of the reader to thyself in penning and perusing these lines, that the highest bliss known on earth may be theirs!

"Our fellowship," said the loving John, "is with the Father and with his Son Jesus Christ." He enjoyed social life. He had his circle of intimate friends. In Jesus he found one worthy of all his love. He followed him joyfully. He heard his counsel with delight. He leaned upon his breast in the hour of formal communion as the child soothes its sorrows in the bosom of its loving mother. When Jesus left this beloved disciple in body they were still together in spirit, and John, like Enoch, walked with God. But John was not alone in this. All believers hold fellowship with the Father and the Son. Some live at home with God, communing with him from day to day. Others return only occasionally to his arms. But all true Christians have more or less of this sweet fellowship. They can say, "Truly, our fellowship is with the Father and with his Son Jesus Christ."

Sometimes there is darkness in the Christian's heart when he has been away from his home. Clouds gather in his horizon. The storm is upon him. All the waves and billows go over him. But the storm does not continue alway. The Sun of Righteousness again arises with healing in his beams. Sad is the state of that man who has no ray of his Father's presence falling upon his heart, no spiritual comfort, no communion with God. The Christian communing with his God, and the unconverted sinner in his native darkness, differ as do two travelers; the one walks cheerfully onward in the bright day-time of spring, through a beautiful landscape, amid cheerful flowers and the joyful songsters of the grove, the spicy breezes fanning his cheeks and the gurgling brooks making music at his side; the other plods his way in darkness, the wild beasts howling around him and thunders reverberating above him. Light is sown for the righteous, but the wicked walk in darkness because they hate the light.

COMMUNION.

CHAPTER I.

MAN'S NEED OF COMMUNION.

THOSE who choose a solitary life are exceptions to the general rule. They are induced to seek retirement from society either from disappointed hopes or from religious fanaticism. Monks and nuns seek separation from society on the ground that they can thereby escape the contamination of the world. But such separation ignores the constitution and instincts of the human mind and heart. Under the pretext of seeking the good of their own souls, these recluses make void the law of love to their neighbors. They are imbedded in the deep of their own selfishness, away from the touch of human sympathy. Spiritual pride generally lies at the foundation of monasteries and convents.

There is also an involuntary separation from society in the solitary confinement of criminals which, for the same reason, may be condemned. It is at war with the sympathies of life. To be shut out from these, to have no word of cheer, no look of affection, no token of regard, is to be like Cain driven out from the presence of God and man. It may well be doubted whether solitary confinement for more than a very short period is proper in any case. Some kind of sympathy is essential to the mental and moral faculties. Bad men need it to reform them, good men need it to make them better. Even paradise itself was incomplete in happiness till man had a companion to share his joys and to commune with him. "It is not good that man should be alone."

The two earliest institutions (arising from the nature and necessities of man) were *marriage* and the *Sabbath*. Marriage was appointed that there might be communion between kindred hearts, and the Sabbath was appointed that there might be time and opportunity for communion with God. Communion with man is not sufficient. Even spiritual communion with man, sweet as it is, does not satisfy the heart. We have need of higher succor. We need some One, in the hour of despondency and grief, that can know all our difficulties, and that can bring relief. We need a Being of infinite love and compassion to stand by us and say, "Fear not, I am with thee." The visible world and human society will not suffice. They cannot always respond to our calls, and when we call their responses are not such as we need. Sometimes their answers chill our hearts, sometimes they mock us with mere promises which are never fulfilled. In the hour of peril they fail us.

> "The friends that in our sunshine live
> When winter comes are flown."

Or if these friends are true and trustworthy, still they do not fully satisfy. As the child playing with its companions becomes weary and often comes back to receive the smiles and caresses of a fond parent, so man is not fully happy in his fellows, but must come, in the intervals of his converse with them, and run to his heavenly Father's arms, or be unhappy. In the sunshine of earthly prosperity he may for a time forget his Maker, his Saviour, but when the night of adversity shuts him out from his business and earthly pleasures, he must nestle, as does the child at night, on a parent's breast.

It affords no objection to this view of the subject that the wicked shun their Maker, that they say to him, " Depart from us, we desire not the knowledge of thy ways." Though they look upon God as their enemy, and therefore seek to hide themselves from his presence, still they feel their need of a friend. Cain did not love God, but when driven out from his presence said that his punishment was greater than he could

2

bear. He needed a friend, but he dared not approach the only one that could forgive, strengthen and comfort him. So it is with all that love not God. They feel that they need a friend, but when God is forced upon their thoughts, as he is by his providence, his word or his Spirit, they resist. The dormant serpent in their breast is warmed into life and activity. The little volcano in their hearts, so long concealed and un-suspected, bursts forth, sometimes into bitter and even profane words of im-patience and rebellion. Sometimes the fire of persecution has been kindled by the fire in their bosoms to consume those who bear the image of God and espouse his cause. But do they not feel their need? Yes, verily. They know themselves to be unhappy, and fear a terrible future. They long for a friend who can give them peace and satisfy the cravings of their souls.

We would gladly convince such that the God whom they so much fear is just the Being whose friendship they need. We would persuade them to come to his mercy-seat. The "seat of dreadful wrath that shot devouring flame" becomes a throne of mercy. Oh, let those that thirst for peace and have it not, who long for a Helper but fear to approach him, remember that God will be their never-failing Friend if they are willing to be reconciled to him. The child of God has found to his joy that his Father smiles upon him. When he has no evidence of this he is troubled. His heart sinks, and he says, "Oh that it were as in days past! Oh that I could again enjoy the presence of my beloved!" "I charge you, O daughters of Jerusalem, if ye find my beloved, that ye tell him that I am sick of love."

Heaven itself would fail to be heaven if our sympathizing Saviour should be absent from the place.

"Not all the harps above
    Would make a heavenly place,
If God his residence remove,
    Or but conceal his face."

What would be the flowers, and green fields, and gushing fountains, and streets of gold, and gates of pearl and rainbow hues, which poetry has ascribed to heaven, were we called to enjoy them alone, or if Jesus were not there to lead us to the fountains of living waters? Heaven would be but a desolation. The longing heart would cry out for fellowship.

Philosophers and others have intellectual communion, and they prize it highly. God is seen in all his works, but his heart is not felt to throb with sympathy and his smile is not seen by the mere philosopher. The heavens are the work of his fingers, his footprints are seen on the earth, and light is his glorious garment. The mountains and seas and tempests are proofs that he has been working. But to look upon all these with the highest admiration does not satisfy the heart longing for sympathy.

A child enters the room of his absent mother. The traces of her work are there. Her sewing is on the stand. Some viands recently prepared are on the table. Her slippers are on the mat. But nothing but the sweet voice and welcoming smile will satisfy the son of her heart. He may partake of the

2 *

food prepared by her hand, he may rest upon the mat beside her slippers, but he is lonesome. The living voice is absent, silence reigns in the hall and no kiss of affection soothes him, for *mother is gone.* So many a philosopher, many a sage, sees the footprints of his Maker in the works which he studies with so much enthusiasm, he even partakes with zest of his bounties and enjoys his gifts; but he has no evidence that God smiles complacently upon him. He runs not to his arms. His heart is desolate.

These learned men who admire God's works, but who have no sweet communion with him in prayer and in his word, are to be pitied. Their Parent is always absent. If they go forward he is not there, if backward they cannot perceive him; on the left hand, where

he doth work, they cannot behold him;
he hideth himself on the right hand,
that they cannot see him. Job xxiii.
8, 9. They see his garments, his footprints, but cannot converse with him.
Astronomy, geology, all the sciences,
show God's handiwork. But we cannot be content with these mere traces
of the great Maker.

> "The ocean's caverns, crags that pierce the sky,
> Majestic trees, the human form erect,
> The worlds on worlds that round about us lie,
> Oh let me look upon the Architect."

Let us come to him, and talk with
him, and hear his kind words of sympathy bidding us trust in him.

CHAPTER II.

THE OBSTACLES TO COMMUNION.

TO deter us from communion with God the law rears its head stern and dark with frowns. The giving of the law was accompanied with clouds and darkness, with thunderings and tempests. Well might Moses say, "I exceedingly fear and quake." And if such terror fell upon a heart so filial and so good, well may unreconciled transgressors quail. Man has broken God's holy law, and how can he come before him? The first effect of a breach of law is to separate the transgressor from his ruler. "The wicked flee when no man pursueth." Adam had no sooner transgressed the law than he sought to hide himself from the presence of the Lord. Thus all transgressors say unto God, "Depart from us: we desire not the knowledge of thy ways."

Look at those two boys. Their father has been absent. When he left home he gave them the parting kiss and bade them to be kind and good till his return. They must not pluck the fruit. They must not wander far away. On his arrival at home one runs to his arms and looks up into his eyes with conscious innocence. The other stands at a distance with downcast eyes, or slinks away from his presence. Why this difference? Ah, the latter has been disobedient; he cannot meet his father's searching eye. He

has broken the law and cannot meet
the lawgiver. He cannot commune
with him while his guilt is upon him.
He separates himself. This seems to
be a universal law, that the transgressor
cannot commune with the ruler. On
this ground Satan was banished from
heaven. On this ground Adam was
driven from paradise, the place where
God had often met with him in loving
converse. For this reason Cain was
driven out from the presence of the
Lord. And on this ground the righteous and wicked will be separated on
the day of judgment, and the wicked
will be separated from God. This will
be "everlasting destruction from the
presence of the Lord and the glory of
his power."

But there cannot be fellowship between the sinner and God, because their

characters are wholly unlike. Even apart from the idea of law and retribution, the natural man cannot have fellowship with God. "What fellowship hath righteousness with unrighteousness? and what communion hath light with darkness? and what concord hath Christ with Belial? or what part hath he that believeth with the infidel? and what agreement hath the temple of God with idols?" Hence the unrenewed cannot enter heaven. "Except a man be born again, he cannot see the kingdom of God." "Can two walk together except they be agreed?" God says of the wicked, "My soul loathed them, and their soul abhorred me."

A plan must therefore be devised to bring parties so estranged together. This was the great problem of the universe. Is there any way of quenching the flames of Sinai? Can the mountains that stand between God and man be removed? "Wherewith shall I come before the Lord, and bow before the Most High God?" What price shall I bring? What deed of merit shall I perform? Tell me, ye angels, if ye have the secret committed to you, how can God be just, and yet receive the sinner? The angels answer not.

CHAPTER III.

THE WAY TO SECURE COMMUNION.

THE angels are silent, but God has spoken! His provision for relief is ample and remarkable. "He will turn again, he will have compassion upon us, he will subdue our iniquities; and thou wilt cast all their sins into the depths of the sea."

To save rebellious man and bring him again to his Father's arms there was early preparation-work in heaven. For removing the great mountains which stood between God and man it required the wisdom and love and power of God. There were two difficulties in the way. The legal difficulty had to be removed by meeting in some way the demands of the law, and man's alienated affections had to be brought back to God.

To remove the first great obstacle, to satisfy the demands of the law, a covenant was entered into by such parties as were certain to keep it. It is called "the covenant of redemption." It is not, perhaps, too fanciful to suppose that a vast assembly was called together (if angels existed before men). God the Father, on his glorious throne, announces to the myriads of beings around him, to thrones, dominions, principalities and powers, that when man shall be created and shall sin, the glorious Son, now present before them in all the greatness of his underived divinity, shall in the fullness of time leave those seats of bliss, shall throw aside those robes of glory and descend to earth, taking upon him the nature of man, there to die, like one of Adam's meanest and vilest children, on the cross of a criminal, suffering unutterable pangs! If Gabriel, in wonder, should ask the reason, we may suppose that God would answer, " Thus far I permit you to know, that sin deserves eternal death, separating the sinner from his Maker for ever. But I seek a reconciliation. I choose to raise many of the fallen race to these beloved seats of bliss where ye now admire, adore and praise. To accomplish this my darling Son must die! I leave you to learn the rest by visiting the earth and the abodes of men, by witnessing the worship of the Jews, their lambs and bullocks bleeding and smoking on the altar, their types and ceremonies pointing to a future Deliverer. Go, when Immanuel shall be born, and announce his birth in songs of praise. Watch him as he grows to manhood, witnessing his spotless life, his violent death, his rising, his ascension, and sing again as you escort him to heaven, 'Lift up your heads, O ye gates, and be ye lifted up, ye everlasting doors, and the King of glory shall come in.' By the utterances of his own lips, and by a preached gospel, and by the millions of converted, redeemed sinners brought back to God, and also by the glorious company of the ransomed met in heaven, when the head of my Son shall be crowned with a diadem of glory, ye shall learn the deep mystery of redemption. Till then, wait in patient expectation."

Accordingly, the world is made and

fitted up as the residence of man, and all the sons of God shout for joy. Man is created in the image of God, and enters upon his endless existence. But, lo! the tempter comes and ruins the first pair, and with them all their posterity. Man becomes a miserable object, a criminal, a rebel, alienated from his God. Could angels weep, they would now drop tears of sorrow. But they listen; words of mysterious import fall upon their ears: "The seed of the woman shall bruise the serpent's head." Soon the blood of animals flows on a thousand altars, betokening some greater sacrifice. As years and centuries roll on the fullness of time arrives. Jesus is born. The angels, having anxiously looked for this event, learn its arrival. All entranced with joy, they sing, "Glory to God in the

3 *

highest, on earth peace, good-will to men." Jesus increases in stature, and at the age of thirty years enters upon his ministerial work. He obeys the law for man. He represents all who believe on him, and for them fulfills all righteousness. The law which man broke he keeps, and as the last great crowning work of his life he bears the sin of man upon the cross, which crushes him down to death. The debt which man owed and could not pay is paid by his great Substitute. Those who receive him as their Saviour are now justified and have peace with God. They can meet him now, and he wears no frown upon his face. Jesus' righteousness is set over to our account, and our debt is paid.

Thus the legal difficulty is removed by our blessed Surety. He became a curse for us. Here is the glorious doctrine of justification. Jesus now sympathizes with us and introduces us again to God's favor and love.

But the other great obstacle must be removed. Man's alienated affections must be brought back to God. The heart must be renewed. This is especially the work of the Holy Spirit. He convinces of sin, he leads to Christ. The work which he commences he carries forward from step to step, till the renewed heart is complete in holiness and made "meet for the inheritance of the saints in light." Our partial sanctification here enables us to enjoy God's presence to some extent. "We see as through a glass, darkly," but we continue to look, and we are drawn as with the cords of love. "We all, with open face beholding as in a glass the glory of the Lord, are changed into the same image, from glory to glory, even as by the Spirit of the Lord." Communion assimilates. The contemplation of divine truth tends to sanctify. Our Saviour prays, "Sanctify them through thy truth; thy word is truth." The sinner, renewed by the Spirit, begins to commune with God. But communion is interrupted by remaining depravity. As this is removed more and more, communion becomes more and more intimate, till, ripe for glory, the Christian goes to dwell in God's presence where is fullness of joy, and at his right hand where are pleasures for evermore. Thus God the Son and God the Holy Spirit co-operate to remove the obstacles in the way of our communion with the Father.

CHAPTER IV.

THE EVIDENCE OF OUR COMMUNION WITH GOD.

NEARLY all our evidences of piety consist in evidences of love to God and communion with him. In prayer, in praise, in reading and hearing God's word, we commune with him. In prayer and praise we talk to God. In our reading and hearing God's word he talks to us. If this converse is sweet to us, we have evidence that we love him. If not, the evidence is against us. If we love the company of any human being, it is an evidence that we love him. So if we love the company of God we love himself.

33

Who can doubt that Mary, who sat at Jesus' feet and heard his words, truly loved her heavenly Friend? Every one now loving to converse with him through the medium of his ordinances is a child of God. Communion is our best evidence of piety. The Lord's Supper is called communion. In this holy ordinance God comes near and talks with us. Do we love to hear him talk? Then we have the evidence of our being his children.

The first Epistle of John dwells much on the evidences of piety. The writer begins by telling us how he had heard and seen and taken by the hand Jesus the word of life. He tells of his continued fellowship with the Father and the Son, and how others might have the same fellowship. He shows that those who walk in darkness, without the light of God's presence, can lay no claim to having fellowship. He shows that obedience gives access to God, and consequently happiness. He says, "We know that we know him if we keep his commandments." As the obedient child is happy in his father's presence, so if we are the obedient children of God we delight in his visits of love. These lessen our attachment to the world, and the world knows us not because it does not know Christ, whose image we bear. We love to commune also with our fellow-Christians. "We know that we have passed from death unto life, because we love the brethren." Here is the communion and fellowship with God and with the brethren spoken of, and we understand thereby our true relation to God. "Love is of God, and every one that loveth is born of God and knoweth God. He that loveth not knoweth not God, for God is love." Again, "Hereby know we that we dwell in him and he in us, because he hath given us of his Spirit." "God is love, and he that dwelleth in love dwelleth in God, and God in him."

Such are the precious teachings of God's word by which we learn that fellowship is the best evidence of our being God's children. Delighting in God's ordinances, in communion, in serving him, in his people, we find that we delight in himself, that we are of his family and preparing to enjoy his heaven.

Next to the first Epistle of John, the Song of Solomon is the book which speaks most of communion. It is a sacred allegory, in which the love and communion of Christ and his Church are set forth under the emblem of the Beloved and his Spouse, with their mutual expressions of endearment and desire for each other's company. They speak each of the other's beauty. They invite each the other to walk in the fields and vineyards.

"My beloved spake," says the spouse, "and said unto me, Rise up, my love, my fair one, and come away. For lo, the winter is past; the rain is over and gone; the flowers appear on the earth; the time of the singing of birds is come and the voice of the turtle is heard in the land. The fig tree putteth forth her green figs, and the vines with the tender grape give a good smell. Arise, my love, my fair one, and come away." She invites him to walk with her in the field and vineyards. "Come,

4

my beloved, let us go forth into the field, let us lodge in the villages. Let us get up early to the vineyards, let us see if the vine flourish, whether the tender grape appear, and the pomegranates bud forth; there will I give thee my loves." She asks him to tell her where he feeds his flock, for she would not turn aside from the same. He calls her to eat and drink with him, and she tells of his bringing her into his banqueting-house, his banner over her being love. She sits under his shadow with great delight, and his fruit is sweet to her taste. In the wilderness she leans upon his arm, and when he withdraws she seeks him, sorrowing till she finds him.

Do we thus love to walk with Jesus, to lean upon him coming up from the wilderness, to follow his flock and feed with them, to enter his banqueting-house, to eat of his precious fruit, to sit under his shadow? Then we have evidence that we are his people. If his absence is painful to us, we have the same evidence.

To be more particular, *faith* is a prominent evidence of our piety. But what is faith? It is a grasping of Christ's hand for help, a leaning upon his arm, like the spouse, upon his bosom, like John. It is a coming to him for peace. It is high communion! Repentance is a prominent evidence. But what is repentance but a return from wandering? What is it but the prodigal coming home to his father's house? What is it but a sorrowing heart seeking solace in One that it has wronged? *Love* is a prominent evidence, but love is the very essence of communion. *New obedience* is an evidence, but new obedience is an obedience flowing from love; it is coming back to God and to duty with a loving, filial heart. *Hope* looks forward to more intimate communion. *Joy* arises from a sense of God's presence. *Peace* is the fruit of reconciliation to God. Thus all Christian graces, all Christian evidences, tend to this one great centre, COMMUNION. Heaven is unalloyed, uninterrupted communion.

If, then, doubting heart, you would know whether you have passed from death unto life, ask whether you love to be with God, to talk with him, to cast your cares upon him, to have him as your chief portion for life, for death, for eternity. Can you say with the Psalmist, "Whom have I in heaven but thee? and there is none on earth that I desire in comparison with thee?" Are the courts of God's house desirable because his presence is there?

On the other hand, are your sorrowful hours those in which your heavenly Friend is absent? Do you cry with Job, " Oh that I knew where I might find him"? Let God be present to my heart and all is well.

4 *

CHAPTER V.

THE HISTORY OF COMMUNION.

TO give the full history of communion would be to reproduce the history of all saints in all ages of the world. It would be to follow every redeemed sinner, from the moment of his conversion, through all the chequered scenes of his earthly pilgrimage, till he basks in the full sunshine of his Saviour's love in heaven. It would be to follow him thither, also, into that everlasting bliss which flows from the presence of his God. But we may look at a few points in this history for our instruction and encouragement.

In paradise, before the Fall, Adam

and Eve had sweet communion with God. They could talk with their Maker as with a loving father who had a heart to beat in unison with theirs. How long they enjoyed the bliss is not on record. Sin drove them from his presence. They sought to hide themselves from Him with whom they had loved to commune.

Enoch "walked with God, and he was not, for God took him." It is altogether probable that the most of his life was spent in intimate fellowship with God. It is expressly said that he walked with God three hundred of the three hundred and sixty-five years of his life. During that long period his advancement in piety must have been great. We may view him as having a joyful and benignant countenance, his eye beaming with hope and his heart gushing with love. As he stepped forth the wicked cowered before him and the righteous greeted him with joy. Children bowed with reverence, yet were not afraid of his approach. It is not strange that God took him to a higher communion. He now walks with God in the full light of heaven.

Of Noah it is also said, "He walked with God." During all the period of that expected storm, and when it came in its terrible fury, sweeping to destruction a wicked world, he was calm and joyful in his God, for he had sheltered himself beneath the wings of everlasting love, and he held sweet converse with his heavenly Father.

Abraham's altars, erected through the land of Canaan, testified how he loved to commune with his covenant God. This made him strong in faith, so that his obedience was unreserved in the most terrible trial.

Isaac meditated at eventide, and also built altars to his father's God.

Jacob wrestled with the Angel of the Covenant, and said to him, "I will not let thee go except thou bless me." He also vowed and said, "*If God will be with me,* and keep me in this way that I go, and will give me bread to eat, and raiment to put on, so that I come to my father's house in peace; then shall the Lord be my God."

Of Joseph it is said, "The Lord was with Joseph." Had he not enjoyed fellowship with God, his trials had certainly crushed his heart.

Moses said to God, "Except thy presence go with me, send us not up thither." God said to him, "My presence shall go with thee, and I will grant thee peace." And he "talked to God face to face, as a man talketh with his friend." Hannah communed with God in secret prayer. David's Psalms breathe the very spirit of fellowship. Listen to his devotions: "In thy presence is fullness of joy; at thy right hand there are pleasures for evermore." "The Lord is my rock, and my fortress, and my deliverer; my God, my strength, in whom will I trust; my buckler and the horn of my salvation and my high tower."

The prophets had communion with God. The apostles enjoyed his presence. Paul was caught up into paradise, and heard unspeakable words. But God communed with him in his daily work also. He could say, "Blessed be the God of all comfort who comforteth us in all our tribulation, that we may be able to comfort them which are in any trouble by the comfort wherewith we are comforted of God."

The martyrs at the stake and in the amphitheatre had the presence of God to such an extent as to enable them to endure the flames and sing praises in death. In all Christian churches, to this hour, God's people have had certain evidence of his presence, while their hearts burned within them as he opened to them the Scriptures and made himself known in the breaking of bread.

But the history of fellowship is only begun. The story can be told by the "just made perfect" in the mansions above when they shall recount together how God in infinite love stooped to lead them through the wilderness below, taking away their griefs and giving them foretastes of the fruit of Canaan.

CHAPTER VI.

THE CONSUMMATION OF COMMUNION.

THE consummation of communion is in reserve. The foretastes are sweet, like the grapes of Eshcol to those traveling to Canaan. But the full feast awaits us in the true Canaan.

Sometimes the gates of heaven are so much "ajar" as to allow the light to come streaming down upon the soul of the believer, especially as his earthly tabernacle is dissolving, but perfect communion is reserved for the light and glory of heaven. If God's children, we have been "delivered from the power of darkness and translated into the kingdom of God's dear Son." But though we live in the kingdom of light, it is in a distant province, and not at the capital where our King resides; he has not yet sent his chariot to take us home. When we arrive at the place of his glorious residence we shall see him as he is. There his people are fully satisfied. "They hunger no more, neither thirst any more, for the Lamb who is in the midst of the throne shall feed them, and lead them to living fountains of water; and God shall wipe away all tears from their eyes." "They follow the Lamb whithersoever he goeth." From the time that they hear the sentence, "Come, ye blessed," there will be the uninterrupted fellowship with Christ and with each other. Jesus now prays for his people: "Father, I will that those whom thou hast given me be with me where I am,

5

that they may behold my glory." "So shall we be ever with the Lord." " In thy presence is fullness of joy, and at thy right hand are pleasures for evermore."

As we get near the throne, "which is to look upon as a jasper and as a sardine stone, and in sight like unto an emerald," the lustre of earthly beauty grows dim. Earthly honors fade. As we hear the "harpers harping with their harps " and the voice of singing as the voice of many waters, all earthly joys will be forgotten. As we turn and gaze upon the Fountain of lights, the brightest earthly glory fades away as stars hide themselves in the light of the rising sun. Fellowship with the Father and his Son Jesus Christ our Lord will be the sunshine of the heart for ever.

Heaven is not merely a rest, it is a rest in God. It is a rest with God's people where they shall see each other and rejoice together in fellowship. Deliverance from conflicts, cares and sins will not be the main ingredient in the cup of enjoyment. Not to be "absent from the body," from pain and sorrow, but to be "present with the Lord," will be the great spring of delight. Whether there will be diversities of tastes and employments among "the white-robed throng" has not been clearly revealed. But "as the cherubim and seraphim are supposed to have their separate and appropriate offices, though all stand round the throne, so may we expect that holy engagements will be distributed in amazing diversity among "the just made perfect." Some may be quicker to discern, others may be more prompt to do. Some may dive deeper into the study of God's attributes, and some into the study of his works, but whatever they study, whatever they do, they cannot wander from their blessed Lord. His presence will furnish the stimulus and fill the cup of their joy.

The communion will not be interrupted by sin or sloth. Here there is much to mar the fellowship of Christians with their Lord and with each other. Those that communed on earth, but often with some degree of coldness and mistrust, will commune without the shadow of a misgiving. Myriads who never met on earth, who never heard of each other, but who were united in one common Lord, shall learn the story of each other's rescue, and conversion, and enjoyments, and struggles, and fears, and hopes on earth, and new friendships will be formed as lasting as eternity.

Methinks I hear the redeemed above conversing about the way in which they were led and sustained and comforted on earth. One tells how he, the chief of sinners, was arrested in his downward career, running away from God and peace; how he was constrained by divine grace to arise and go to his Father, who received the wanderer with affectionate embrace. Another tells how he walked with God when all earthly sympathy failed him. Another recounts his joyful communion seasons, when Jesus took him into his banqueting-house and his banner over him was love. Another tells how Jesus met him as darkness gathered over his eyes, as heart failed, as the lungs ceased to

5 *

receive the vital air, as he sank away in the embrace of death; how his Saviour whispered in his ear, "Fear not, I am with thee; be not dismayed, for I am thy God." Thus telling and hearing of themes of the past, they strike their harps and sing: "To Him that loved us and washed us from our sins in his own blood be honor and power, praise and dominion for ever." Jesus and his salvation are the beginning and close of every song.

But we speak as children, childishly, when we speak of the communion of heaven. We see "through a glass, darkly," but we shall see "face to face." Let us labor to enter into that rest lest any of you should seem to come short of it.

CHAPTER VII.

THE LORD'S SUPPER.

THERE is one observance in the Christian Church which more than any other cements Christian love and foreshadows the communion in glory. It is called by various names, but " communion " expresses its true object. It is the outward act by which the love and fellowship and flowing together of the heart of Christ and his people are represented and increased.

Jesus has gone to his Father, and we cannot take him by the hand, or look into his loving eyes, or lean, like John, upon his breast, or anoint his feet, like

Mary; but we can touch and taste and look upon those emblems which he has himself appointed to remind us of his love and of the place which we hold in his heart. In this holy communion Jesus sheds his graces into our hearts and comforts us with a sense of his spiritual presence. At his invitation we seat ourselves beside him, and he talks with us there. By his word and Spirit he abides with us, and by faith we abide with him. We commemorate what he has done and felt for us. We join ourselves to him in covenant and promise that his interest shall be our interest, that we will henceforth have with him but one aim, one mind, one joy.

There is communion with all the saints, whether they are seated with us at the table or otherwise. There is communion with "all that in every place call on the name of Jesus Christ our Lord, both theirs and ours." He is their Lord, our Lord, the common Lord of all believers, and recognized as such in the communion.

God's people are dispersed over the world. They cannot all meet together at one place. But though scattered and separated into different denominations, they commune together. They cannot do otherwise. The Spirit of their Master is in them all. They are united to him by a living faith, and are branches of the same vine, and have a common life. If they build up walls of separation and say to one another, "You cannot commune with us," still the Spirit unites them, and they cannot be separated. Nay, all the saints above have fellowship with all the saints below, and there is but one communion. Visible communion can be broken, but the invisible cannot. As neither life, nor death, nor things present, nor things come to pass, can separate God's people from his love, so no bars put up by Christians can separate them spiritually from each other. The fruit on this side of the wall cannot say to the fruit on that side of the wall borne by the same vine, "We are separated and have no communion." The wall is a dead thing, while the vine and all the clusters, wherever they hang, are pervaded by the same life.

Christians are all united by the same covenant and stamped with the image and superscription of Jesus Christ. In the Lord's Supper we "drink into one spirit."

The question of "open communion"

and " close communion " is affected by these considerations. Open communion is the free flow of the sap of the vine into the various branches. Close communion is an attempt to prevent or hinder that free flow. Close communion intimates or asserts that the sap flowing into some branches is richer or more nourishing than that flowing into others. Those practicing close communion seem to bandage their own branch to prevent the sap of the common trunk from flowing freely. They thus check their own growth and fruitfulness.

The blood of the human body must flow freely to all the limbs, or there are paralysis and death. The assumption of close communion is an assumption that the other members do not belong to the body. And yet the most prejudiced will not advocate this doctrine.

They preach with others, they pray with others, they build no barrier between themselves and others, except in the matter of sitting together at the Lord's table—that thing which indicates the very life-flow of the Church. They will allow the nerves of the body to vibrate together, but not the blood of the body to flow together.

If there is any ordinance in which evangelical Christians should unite, it is the Lord's Supper. This is not an ordinance which should be used as a testimony against error. Let testimony be borne in preaching, but a sacrament whose very design is to draw Christian hearts together cannot be a testimony against Christians. Refusal to commune implies that there is not a common Christian life. So we do refuse to commune with the ungodly world, with those who deny the divinity of Christ, with those who hold to fatal error. And if we refuse to commune with our brethren of other evangelical denominations, we put them in the same category. We say they are not the children of God. Though we may not mean to make so strong an assumption, it is virtually made.

It is said that discipline cannot be maintained if we allow all to commune who are in regular standing in other evangelical churches—that we thus receive to our communion persons who could not be taken into our own particular church. But we receive them to the Lord's table by virtue of their connection with churches over which we have no control. Theirs is the responsibility of retaining unworthy members. We are not responsible for the communing

of unconverted members, whether in
our own congregation, in another congregation in our own connection, or in
a church of a different denomination.
We may and ought to prune our own
branches that they may be more fruit-
ful. But the neglect of others to
prune does not separate the whole
branch from the vine. We do not
sanction any of the errors of other
churches by intercommunion, unless
those errors strike at the foundation of
our religion, unless they tend to uproot
the vine itself.

In our own church there may be
false professors or those whose walk is
not consistent, and if we will not commune till the church is rid of these, we
shall for ever stand aloof from the
Lord's table. Discipline should be en-
forced by the proper authorities, but

we should not refuse to commune, and thus separate ourselves from Christ and his people, because there are unworthy members in the church.

We may ask, What are the proper qualifications for coming to the Lord's table? This question has pressed many hearts with a load of intense solicitude, and many answers have been given to it. The writer would direct the inquirer's thoughts to a view of this subject falling in with the general tenor of this book. Let the reader turn back to Chapter IV., *The Evidences of Communion.* But that he may be more fully in possession of a method of self-examination let him consider prayerfully the following questions. If he can honestly answer them in the affirmative, he has reason to consider himself a child of God, and entitled to a place with God's people in visible communion. These questions are similar to those written by Dr. Griffin for the use of the students of Williams College more than forty years ago.

Do I love God? Do I love him for his holiness, justice and purity, as well as for his pardoning mercy? Am I glad that he is displeased with sin, even my sins, though he will pardon them through Christ? Am I glad that God orders all things, and my interests as well as those of others? Am I submissive to his will in affliction, knowing that he acts the part of a kind Father in chastening his child? Do I love to approach him in prayer, in praise, in reading and hearing his word? Can I entrust all my interests into his hands for this world and the next? Do I depend upon him for all needful grace to do the work required of me? Do I greatly desire to see God honored by all men? Do I wish and determine to serve him for ever? Do I love to commune with him in prayer? Is it sweet to come to him and call him Father? Am I thankful to God for life and its comforts, for his presence and promises? Do I feel incapable of making any compensation to God for his love and favor?

Do I love God's law? Am I glad that he requires me to love him with all my powers, and my neighbor as myself? Do I hate sin because it is against a good and holy God, and separates from him? Do I wish more to be free from sin than from poverty, sickness or any earthly affliction? Do I long for holiness? Is indwelling sin a burden to me? Am I sorry for heart sins as well as sins more outward and

6 *

known to others? Do I love to repent?

Have I, under a sense of my sins, cast myself upon Jesus for salvation? Do I believe that Jesus is the only Saviour, and an all-sufficient Saviour? Do I believe that his blood is sufficient to wash away the greatest sin? Do I come to him for forgiveness? Do I renounce all merit, and seek to be saved by grace alone? *Do I really depend upon Jesus' death as the ground of my pardon?* Do I hope for all good through his merits and prayers? Do I feel that I may go to God through Christ, vile as I am? Do I desire that all others should come and be saved? Is Christ precious to my soul? Do I count other things as dross in comparison with him? Does the cross crucify me to sin and the world? Do I feel that I am not my own, but bought with a price for God?

Do I feel that I am dependent upon the Holy Spirit for all good desires? Do I try to avoid grieving the Spirit? Do I desire to be led by the Spirit? Do I ask him to enlighten, quicken and comfort me? Do I love the Lord's day? Do I love religious exercises? Do I love God's people? Am I trying to do right in every respect?

CHAPTER VIII.

PRAYER IN VIEW OF COMMUNION, OR COMING TO THE LORD'S TABLE.

For the removal of obstacles to communion.

MOST merciful God, thou hast taught me to call thee by the endearing name of Father. Why then hidest thou thy face from me? Why standest thou afar off? When I cry, thou shuttest out my prayer. Alas, my sins have separated between thee and me, and caused thee to hide thy face from me. Against thee, thee only, have I sinned. Thy law is holy, just and good, but I have broken it. How canst thou be pleased with me, a vile transgressor? Thou art the best of Rulers, and I have been a rebellious subject. Thou art the kindest of Fathers, and I have been a disobedient child. Thou hast been unwearied in thy care, and I have been full of ingratitude. But thou hast borne with me and not cut me off. It is of thy mercies that I am not consumed. Thou hast in kindness invited me to return to thee. How may I come? How can this heart be reconciled to God? How can I come to an offended Father? Wherewith shall I come before the Lord and bow before the Most High God? Lord, teach me the way; show me thy paths. Take away the barriers by which I am shut out from thy presence. Let not the law terrify me and drive me from thy face. O Lord, rebuke me not in thine anger, neither chasten me in thy hot displeasure. Hast thou not laid help upon One who is mighty to save? Look, then, upon Jesus, who gave his soul a sacrifice for sin. Remember his perfect righteousness. Save me, a poor sinner, through his blood. O Lord, I plead before thee the atonement as the ground of my acceptance. Clinging to the cross, thy justice will not smite me. The sword of vengeance cannot reach me here. It is here that I come and plead for pardon and salvation through the blood of Jesus. Blessed be thy name! thou art on thy mercy-seat. Thou hearest the cry of the desolate. Come, O Lord, and save me, for Jesus' sake. Leave me not in darkness without the tokens of thy presence. Remove the corruptions of my heart that I may have fellowship with thee.

Take from me all my transgressions

and own me as thy child. Whisper peace to this weary heart, and I will love and praise thee. Prepare me to come with thy people and sit as an accepted guest at thy table. Now, O Lord, accept my poor petitions through Jesus Christ my Saviour. Amen.

On going to the Lord's table.

Thy people, O Lord, are about to gather around the sacred board and celebrate the love of our blessed Lord. Make me a welcome guest with them. Put upon me the wedding garment, the robe of righteousness. I will come in my Saviour's perfect robe. Clothed in this pure garment, thou wilt bid me welcome. But what am I that I should have communion with my brethren, my Saviour, my heavenly Father? I am unworthy of this high privilege, for I have forfeited it by my sins. But it is to sinners that thou givest these great privileges. As a sinner I come and claim that Jesus died for sinners. God be merciful to me, a sinner! Grant me the tokens of thy love, and be reconciled to me through Jesus Christ. Bless all thy people who are about to commune together. May we all be of one heart and one soul! May our fellowship be with the Father and with his Son Jesus Christ! Enable us to love one another with a pure heart fervently. And make this communion a foretaste of the communion above, for Christ's sake. Amen.

THE END.